KU-250-810

Allison Douglas

My Own
FAIRYTALE
BOOK

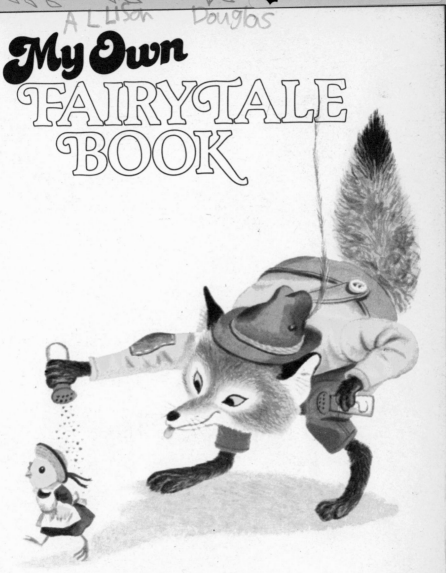

Hamlyn
London · New York · Sydney · Toronto

This edition first published 1978 by
The Hamlyn Publishing Group Limited
Astronaut House, Hounslow Road, Feltham, Middlesex.
Copyright © 1960, 1959, 1955, 1954, 1953 Western
Publishing Company, Inc., Racine, Wisconsin, U.S.A.

ISBN 0 600 36296 5

Printed in Italy

Contents

Three Favourite Stories

Puss-in-Boots
Cinderella
The Sleeping Beauty

Illustrated by Gertrude Elliot

Puss-in-Boots

'Give me a pair of boots and a sack,' Puss said to his master, one day, 'and I will make your fortune.'

His master who knew of no way to make his own fortune, since he was just a poor miller's son, gave Puss what he had asked for.

Puss put on his boots, and was called Puss-in-Boots from that day on. He put a handful of grain in the sack and went off into the forest.

He put the sack down and quietly waited nearby. A young rabbit soon hopped up and into the sack, and very quickly Puss-in-Boots tightened the cord round the top. He had captured the rabbit which he then took to the king's palace.

He was taken to see the king to whom he presented the rabbit, saying, 'This is a present for you from the Marquis of Carabas,' – a name Puss-in-Boots had made up for his poor young master.

In the days that followed Puss-in-Boots took many gifts to the king, always in the name of the Marquis of Carabas.

One day Puss learnt that the king would be taking his daughter for a ride in the royal carriage along the banks of the river. Quickly he ran to his master. 'Be sure to bathe in the river this afternoon. It will help me to make your fortune.'

So, just as Puss had suggested, his master was swimming in the river as the king's carriage came into sight. Puss ran towards it crying, 'Quickly, please save the Marquis of Carabas! He is drowning!'

The name, by now, was familiar to the king. He cried to the footmen, 'Save the Marquis of Carabas!'

Then, Puss told the king that robbers had stolen his master's fine clothes.

The king sent for the finest set of clothes to be brought from his palace for the Marquis of Carabas, and they all rode back towards the palace together. Puss-in-Boots was well ahead of them.

Soon Puss arrived at a beautiful castle which he knew was owned by an ogre. Puss-in-Boots strolled through the main entrance and when he saw the ogre said, 'Rumour has it that you can change yourself into any animal you choose – say a lion or a mouse. Is it true?'

13

The ogre was always keen to display his cleverness, and so he changed himself immediately into a lion. Then the next second he was an ogre again. 'How about changing into a mouse now?' asked Puss.

The ogre agreed and once again changed his appearance. Puss-in-Boots pounced on the mouse and that was the end of the ogre! The castle was free at last.

Puss-in-Boots ran downstairs, and threw open the castle gates, just as the royal coach was approaching.

'Welcome to the castle of the Marquis of Carabas!'

When the king saw the splendour of the castle he was sure the Marquis of Carabas was a great man, and was delighted to agree to a marriage for his beautiful daughter, who had already fallen in love with the miller's son.

So, Puss-in-Boots had indeed made his master's fortune and his own, too!

Cinderella

Once upon a time there was a pretty young girl who was made to do all the hardest work in the house in which she lived.

She had two ugly sisters who used to laugh at her and call her Cinderella because every day they made her clear away the cinders from the large fireplace.

It happened that one day the king's son was giving a grand ball to which Cinderella's ugly sisters had been invited. Cinderella was left behind, and she felt so unhappy that she cried.

But suddenly her fairy godmother appeared and smiling kindly she waved her wand and said, 'Cinderella, you shall go to the ball!' At once, her patched, torn old dress, was turned into a beautiful dress of white satin, and on her feet she wore two dainty glass slippers. Another wave of the wand, and the fairy godmother changed a pumpkin into a golden coach. Finally she transformed four mice that were scurrying across the floor into four horses that could pull the

golden coach. Cinderella was speechless with delight as she climbed into her seat.

'Take great care to leave the ball before the clock strikes midnight, because that is when the spell will be broken,' said the fairy godmother as the horses pulled away.

When Cinderella arrived at the ball a silence fell as she entered the room.

'Who is this beautiful girl?' everyone asked.

The prince could look only at Cinderella, and throughout the whole evening he danced with no-one else. Cinderella was so happy that she forgot how quickly time was passing. She had forgotten her fairy godmother's warning. Suddenly the clock chimed the first stroke of midnight.

Startled, Cinderella ran out of the ballroom and out of the palace. The prince ran after her but all he found was one of Cinderella's glass slippers which she had lost on her way down the staircase.

Cinderella arrived home with not one sign of the splendour in which she had departed for the ball. There was no golden carriage, no horses, no beautiful dress – just the one glass slipper left behind at the palace in the prince's possession.

The prince was so in love with the girl he had danced with all evening, that he announced that he would marry the girl whose foot fitted the little glass slipper.

So he and his servants took the slipper to all the princesses, the duchesses, and every woman at the court, but it was no good. It did not fit any of them. At last they came to Cinderella's house. The two ugly sisters tried to fit the little slipper on to their feet but it was much too small.

Cinderella was looking on and she recognized the slipper. She laughed and said, 'Who knows, perhaps it will fit me!' The ugly sisters scorned her, but one of the prince's servants said that she must try on the slipper since he had been told that every girl must try it. As soon as Cinderella put on the slipper, it was clear that it fitted her perfectly. The two sisters were very angry and even more surprised when Cinderella took the other slipper from her pocket.

Then her fairy godmother arrived, and with a touch of her wand, Cinderella's clothes changed into those that she had worn at the ball. They took her to the palace where the prince recognized her at once. He thought she was more beautiful than ever, and so a few days later they were married and they lived happily ever after.

The Sleeping Beauty

Once upon a time there was a little princess, and the king and queen invited the five good fairies to her christening. The bad fairy was not invited.

The castle shone with lights in honour of the ceremony, lit with a thousand candles. A wonderful banquet was given and the food was served on golden plates.

That evening the good fairies gathered around the crib. They bestowed the most wonderful gifts upon the baby princess. One gave intelligence, another great beauty, the third bestowed grace, then the fourth good fairy gave her joy.

Just as the fourth fairy had made her gift, the window was flung open and in came the bad fairy, dressed all in black.

She scowled at the good fairies and bent over the baby princess, her face full of anger.

'I also have a gift,' she muttered. 'On your fifteenth birthday you will prick your finger on a spinning wheel, and you will die!'

These terrible words made everyone tremble, and the king and queen began to cry.

The fifth fairy moved towards the crib. 'There is no need to worry,' she said gently. 'I have not yet made my gift. It is true that I cannot change everything, but the princess will not die when she pricks her finger on the spinning wheel. She will only fall into a deep sleep and remain so for a hundred years.'

The king, who wanted to avoid the accident happening at all, made a proclamation forbidding anyone to keep a spinning wheel, under pain of death.

But, on the day of her fifteenth birthday, the princess was exploring an old part of the castle when she found a winding staircase that led up to a little room in the top of one of the towers. Inside the room an old woman was using a spinning wheel.

The princess had never seen one before and immediately asked, 'Oh, please let me try! I've never seen a spinning wheel before.'

She sat down on the stool which the old woman had been using, and no sooner had she bent over the spinning wheel than she pricked her finger, just as the bad fairy had predicted.

Almost immediately she fell to the floor in a deep sleep. But not only did the princess sleep – all the people in the palace fell asleep, too. Even the horses slumbered in the stables. And over the years the bushes and brambles grew so thickly around the palace that it became hidden from view.

When a hundred years had passed, a prince happened to pass by. He had no idea that the tangle of brambles concealed a castle, then to his astonishment a pathway opened up before him. Soon he came up to the main entrance of the castle. He entered, climbed the stairs and found Sleeping Beauty. He bent over her and kissed her gently and from that moment the spell was broken! Sleeping Beauty woke up and immediately fell in love with the handsome prince. And at the same time, everyone else in the palace started to stir. All the stable boys and housemaids and cooks and the king and queen.

Sleeping Beauty and the prince had fallen in love at first sight, and the king and queen were overjoyed to consent to their marriage.

That night the palace was lit once again by a thousand candles and there was a great celebration at the castle that had come to life again.

The Brave Little Tailor

By the
Brothers Grimm

Illustrated by
J. P. Miller

There was once a little tailor who loved bread and jam.
He munched it while he worked every day. But one day
some hungry flies swarmed in, and they nibbled at his
bread and jam too.

That made the little tailor very angry. 'Shoo!' he
cried. 'I'll get rid of you!' Swat! he went with a length of
cloth.

Down fell the flies – four, five, six, seven of them,
dead as so many dry leaves!

'Ho!' laughed the tailor. 'Seven at one blow!'

This sounded so pleasing, that he stitched the words
upon a belt and clasped it around his waist.

Then, feeling pleased with himself, he closed his shop, and for a treat he bought himself a piece of cheese. Before he could eat it, he heard a faint noise. Close beside his feet lay an exhausted bird.

Stuffing the cheese into his pocket, the kind-hearted tailor picked up the bird, smoothed its ruffled feathers and tucked it gently into another pocket.

Then off marched the little tailor, cocky as could be, with his thumbs thrust through his belt.

Soon he met a giant resting beside a tree.

'Good day, comrade,' the cheery tailor said. 'How would you like to have my company?'

'You!' roared the giant. 'What would I want with a little pipsqueak like you?'

'Perhaps,' said the tailor, 'you don't know my worth.' And he turned around slowly to let the giant read the 'Seven at one blow' stitched on his belt.

'Hm,' said the giant, of course thinking it was men the tailor had laid out with his one blow. 'I'll test your strength. Let me see you do this.' He picked up a stone and squeezed it in his hand until a drop of water ran out.

'Is that all?' laughed the tailor, pulling out his piece of cheese. He squeezed till the whey ran down in a stream.

'Hm,' said the giant, with a frown. 'Match this now, if you can!' picking up another stone, he threw it so high that the eye could scarcely see it before it plunged back to earth.

'Is that all?' laughed the tailor. 'Mine will not come

back at all.' He felt in his pocket, brought out the bird, and tossed it up into the air. Away it flew, far out of sight, and the giant grumbled with a thunder-roar when he saw that he was beaten.

'Let's see you lift a weight,' the giant said, hoisting to his shoulder the trunk of a fallen oak. 'Help me carry this tree if you can.'

'Gladly,' said the tailor. 'You take the little trunk. I will carry the big branching top.'

Away went the giant, staggering under his load. Up into the branches the tailor hopped and whistled a tune as he rode along.

'Whew!' gasped the giant after a while. 'That is enough for me.' He set down the trunk with a thud.

SEVEN

33

'Ho!' laughed the tailor, swiftly hopping down. 'It didn't seem heavy at all to me.' The giant was angry, but he tried to hide his rage.

'Come home and spend the night with my partner and me,' he said. 'My partner will be glad to meet a sturdy little fellow like you.'

'Gladly,' said the tailor. So home they went to the giant's gloomy cave.

After a huge supper, the two giants showed the brave little tailor to a giant-sized bed and said goodnight to him. But the tailor could not sleep in that huge bed, so he curled up in a corner.

In the middle of the night, he heard footsteps close by. Opening one eye, the little tailor saw the giants tiptoe up to the empty bed and pound it all over with great clubs. Then, satisfied that the little tailor was

done for at last, they went back to the fireside and soon were sound asleep.

The brave little tailor waited till they snored. Then he dropped a dish on the head of one.

'Stop hitting me!' that giant grumbled, pushing at his partner sleepily.

'I didn't hit you,' the partner said. But just then the little tailor dropped a dish on his head. 'Hey, you stop hitting me!' he cried, ramming an elbow sharply into his partner's chest.

Soon they were fighting for all they were worth, until in the end they tore each other to bits.

The brave tailor watched from his safe corner, and when nothing was left of those mean old giants, he marched proudly out of that cave and back to his home town.

He found the town in a great uproar because of those giants and the wicked things they had done. The king had offered his daughter in marriage to anyone who could free the land of them.

'Oho!' cried the tailor. 'The princess is mine! I killed those old giants last night.'

No one believed him. Everyone laughed at the cocky, boasting little tailor.

'Go and see!' said the tailor. So the king sent his army out to the cave.

They came back with the news that the tailor spoke the truth. 'And oh, what a battle it must have been!' they cried.

So the tailor won the hand of the princess that day, and as much bread and jam as he wished.

Thumbelina

By Hans Christian Andersen

Illustrated by Gustaf Tenggren

There was once a tiny little girl. She was sweet and pretty and no taller than your thumb, so she was called Thumbelina.

A nicely varnished walnut shell made a bed for her, with a violet petal mattress and a rose leaf coverlet.

That was where she slept at night; but in the daytime she played in a small garden made in a bowl, where she rowed her tulip-petal boat from side to side of a tiny flower-wreathed lake.

One night as she lay in her pretty bed, a large ugly toad came hopping in through the open window, and jumped straight to the table where Thumbelina was lying asleep.

'She would make just the wife for my son,' thought the toad. So she snatched up Thumbelina, walnut shell and all, and hopped off with her, back to the garden.

There, in the muddy bank of a wide brook, the toad made her home with her ugly son. There the mother toad left Thumbelina in her walnut shell bed, on a water-lily leaf, floating on the brook.

In the morning, when the poor little thing woke up,
and saw where she was, she cried most bitterly. For the
big green leaf had water all around it, so she could not
possibly escape.

The little fishes, swimming in the water below, heard
her crying. So they all swam around the tough green
stalk that held Thumbelina's leaf, and they tugged at it
until it broke.

Then away the leaf floated with Thumbelina on it, far away down the brook, where the toad could never reach her.

For a while the journey was pleasant, for she was sailing through a lovely, open part of the brook. But when her leaf boat swirled to a stop against a mossy bank, Thumbelina found herself alone in a strange forest world.

There was no way she could travel further, so all through the summer Thumbelina lived quite alone in that enormous wood. She wove a bed from blades of grass. She hung it neatly under a leaf, so that she was sheltered from the rain.

For food she had honey from the flowers, for drink, the morning dew on the leaves. And so she passed the summer and autumn.

Then came winter – the bitter winter, and as Thumbelina searched for a warmer shelter, it began to snow.

She came at last to a door on the fringe of the wood,

where down below the stubble of a large cornfield, a
field mouse had a fine snug house.

'You poor little thing!' said the kindly field mouse,
when she found Thumbelina shivering at her door.
'Come into my warm room and eat with me.'

The mouse took a liking to Thumbelina at once, and
invited her to stay for the winter. Thumbelina agreed,
and was comfortable there.

In the evenings the field mouse's neighbour often
came to call. He was a tiresome old mole.

'But his house is even snugger than mine,' the mouse
said, 'and he wears such a lovely black velvet coat. If
only you could get him for a husband, you'd be well off
indeed!'

Thumbelina paid no attention to this. She had no
intention of marrying the mole. He was very learned,
she agreed, but he couldn't bear sunshine and flowers.

Now he had dug a long passage from his house to theirs, and there one day Thumbelina found a bird – a swallow, numb with cold and almost dead.

She wove a fine big blanket of hay, and she spread it over the swallow and tucked some sheep's wool in at the sides. She brought him water in the petal of a flower, and took care of him all winter long.

When she was not caring for the swallow,
Thumbelina spent her time spinning and weaving her
wedding clothes, for the tiresome mole had proposed to
her, and the mouse decided they should be married
soon.

Poor Thumbelina! She grew sadder and sadder.

When spring arrived, bringing her wedding day, and
the sun began to warm the earth, Thumbelina opened a

hole in the roof of the passage, and the swallow flew out into the welcome sunshine.

Thumbelina watched him with tears in her eyes.

'Come with me, Thumbelina,' he begged, for he could not bear to let her marry the mole and live forever underground.

'Yes,' said Thumbelina at once, 'I will come with
you.' So she climbed on the bird's back and the swallow
flew high up into the air, over lakes and forests, high up
over the mountains of everlasting snow.

At last they reached the warm countries, where
grapes grew on sunny walls and slopes, and lemons and
oranges ripened in the groves.

The swallow flew on, while the country became more
and more beautiful, until at last they came to an ancient
palace of shining marble, standing among green trees

beside a blue lake. Here the swallow flew down with Thumbelina.

He placed her on a broad flower petal – and there, in the middle of the flower, was a little man no bigger than herself. He was the king of the spirits of the flowers.

'Oh! how handsome he is!' Thumbelina thought. And the little king was equally enchanted at the sight of her. He took the crown from his own head and placed it on hers. Then he asked her what she was called, and if she would be his wife.

She knew at once he was the husband for her, so she
said, 'Yes' to the king. Then from every flower round
about tiny people like herself appeared. Each of
them brought a gift for the new queen, but her favourite
was a pair of beautiful wings from a white butterfly.
These they fastened to her back, so that she could flit
with the others from flower to flower.

Such rejoicing as there was then! And the swallow sat in his nest above and sang for their happiness with all his loving heart.

The Twelve Dancing Princesses

By the Brothers Grimm
retold by Jane Werner

Illustrated by Sheilah Beckett

A poor soldier was homeward bound from the wars. He was looking for a place to settle down where he might make his fortune.

Then he was told about the king of the country, who had twelve daughters, each lovelier than the next. To guard them from harm, he locked the door of their room in the palace at bedtime each night. Yet every morning, as sure as the dawn, beside each bed in that locked

room stood a pair of dancing slippers worn quite
through. But no one could say where the princesses had
been.

So the king offered a reward – the hand of the
princess of his choice and the right to inherit the throne,
to any young man who could learn the secret of the
dancing princesses. But if, within three days and three
nights, he did not learn the secret, the young man
would die.

'Ho,' said the soldier, 'this is just the thing for me.'
So he set off for the king's palace.

He met an old woman along the way, who asked,
'Where are you bound, young man?' 'I'm off to learn
the secret of the dancing princesses,' he replied
laughing.

'That should not be too hard,' the old woman said, 'if
you remember not to drink anything they offer you at
night.'

Then from her pocket she pulled out a cloak which
she put in the soldier's hand.

'Put this around your shoulders,' she told him, 'and you will be invisible. You can follow the princesses and see what happens.'

The soldier thanked her heartily, and went on with all speed to the court of the king.

'You may start tonight,' said the weary king. And he had the soldier shown to a bed set up just beside the princesses' room.

At bedtime the eldest princess brought him a hot
drink, and the soldier took it eagerly. But he did not
drink it; he let the hot milk run down into a sponge he
wore tied beneath his shirt. Then he stretched himself
out upon his bed and pretended to sleep.

When the princesses heard him snoring away, they
ran to their wardrobes and brought out pretty dresses,
and they decked themselves for a ball.

Then the eldest princess tapped her bed and it sank into the floor. In its place a great trapdoor appeared, through which they all disappeared.

Quickly the soldier sprang up, pulled on his cape, and all unseen he followed them, so close that he stepped on the youngest girl's dress.

'Who is stepping on my dress?' she cried.

'You caught it on a nail, silly; there is no one there,' the older princesses said.

So on they went, down the long flight of stairs, with the unseen soldier close behind.

At the bottom of the steps he found himself in an avenue of trees with tinkling silver leaves.

'I must take one back with me,' the soldier thought. So he broke off a silver twig.

Crack! went the twig – and the youngest princess jumped. Again the others laughed at her.

Soon they reached the shore of a lake, where twelve little boats were lined up. In each of the boats waited a handsome prince. One princess leaped into each small boat, handed down by the waiting prince; and the soldier too stepped into the last, and sat beside the youngest princess.

At last the boats reached the far side of the lake where a splendid castle stood.

There the princes danced with their princesses until holes appeared in the ladies' dainty shoes. Then back to the lake they sadly went, and into the boats again.

This time the soldier rode with the eldest princess, and he sprang ashore first. While the young folk were saying fond goodnights, he sprang up the stairway, into the bedroom, and was sound asleep on his bed, or so it seemed, when the twelve princesses returned.

'We are safe,' said the princesses when they found
him there, and they put their pretty ball gowns away,
tucked their worn-out slippers under their beds, and
went to sleep themselves.

Next day the soldier said nothing. But that night he followed them again, and the third night also. Then he brought back a jewelled cup from the castle, under his cloak.

So at last his final morning arrived; he was called before the king. The princesses sat beside their father, trying to hide their smiles.

'Where do my daughters dance at night?' the king asked, looking very stern.

'At an underground castle beside a lake,' the soldier answered, 'with a dozen handsome princes.' Then he

told the whole story to the king, and he showed him the
twig with the silver leaves, and brought out the jewelled
cup he had taken from the castle itself.

'Is this true?' roared the angry king to the princesses,
and they saw they could no longer deny it.

'Well, which of them will you have for a wife?' the
king asked the soldier, when the princesses had
confessed.

'I am no longer young,' the soldier said. 'Give me the
eldest for my bride.'

The wedding was celebrated that very day, and the soldier was made the heir to the throne. So the soldier had found his fortune indeed.

But do you know that not one of those handsome princes from underground came to dance on his wedding day?

By the Brothers Grimm

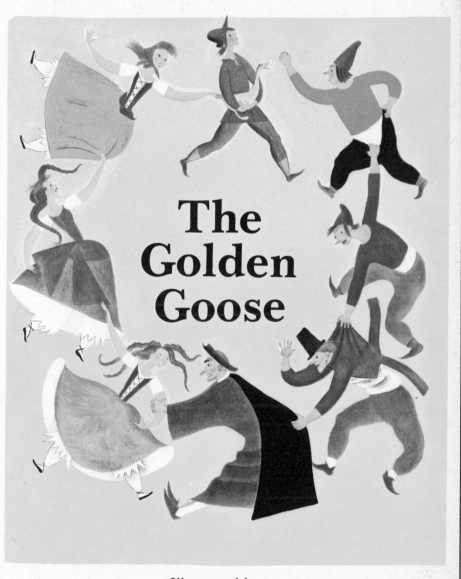

The Golden Goose

Illustrated by
Gustaf Tenggren

There was once a woodcutter who had three sons. The first and second sons were considered bright young men. But the youngest was treated most unkindly, for everyone thought him a stupid boy. Because of this he was called Dozey.

One day the two older brothers took plenty of food and went into the wood to cut fuel. They had not gone far when a little old man stopped them.

'I beg you, share some of your lunch with me, for I am hungry and thirsty,' he said.

But the brothers replied, 'If we feed you we shall have less for ourselves.' With that they went to chop their fuel. But before long the axe slipped, and they

both cut their arms. So they trudged home with
bandaged arms and no wood at all.

So the next day, Dozey went off to cut some wood,
with very little food and only a cup of water. He too met
the old man, who asked him for a bite to eat.

'What's mine is yours,' said Dozey cheerily. And they
sat down together to share Dozey's lunch.

'You have a kind heart and have shared all you had. .
In return I will send you a blessing which will make
your fortune. Dig under that tree there and you will find
something at the root.' And with that he disappeared.

Dozey dug with a will and there he found a goose
with feathers of the purest gold!

Dozey tucked the goose under his arm and set out to seek his fortune. He stopped that night at an inn, taking his precious goose with him.

When the innkeeper's three daughters saw the golden
goose each decided that, come what would, she must
have a shining feather for her own.

First the eldest sister slipped into Dozey's room. Quietly she reached for a feather. But no sooner did she touch the goose than she found herself stuck to it, and unable to move at all!

Next the second sister crept into Dozey's room, jealously determined that her sister should not get all the feathers. But lo and behold! the moment she touched her sister, she, too, stuck fast.

At last the youngest sister sneaked in. But the other two cried out, 'Keep away! For goodness sake, keep away!

'Why should I keep away while they get the golden feathers?' thought the foolish girl. And in a twinkling she was fastened as tightly as her sisters.

Next morning, Dozey picked up his goose and set off, taking no notice at all of the three girls. But wherever he went they, too, were forced to follow.

Before long an old parson saw the strange procession.

'Aren't you ashamed to follow this young man?' he
called to the girls. And he took the youngest by the
hand to lead her away. But as soon as he touched her,
he, too, was stuck fast.

By and by the clerk passed by and was amazed to see
his master, the parson, running after the three girls.

'Hi, Master!' he called. 'Where are you going?' And
he grabbed the parson's gown. When, bless my soul! He
stuck fast too!

In this way the five of them travelled until they
passed two farmers working in a field.

'Help us, help us!' shouted the parson and the clerk.

'Help us, help us!' cried the three sisters. But no sooner did the farmers lay hands on the clerk to pull him away, than they, too, fell into the ranks and all seven ran after Dozey and his goose!

It so happened that in the town through which Dozey and his companions travelled there lived a beautiful princess who had neither laughed nor smiled for three

years. The worried king had offered her hand in
marriage and half the kingdom, to anyone who could
make her laugh.

On this day the unhappy princess was looking out of
her window. Suddenly she saw Dozey and his strange
train of followers.

As she watched them stumbling and tripping after
each other, her face broke into a smile. And soon she
was laughing until the tears rolled down her cheeks.

So Dozey got half the kingdom and married the princess as well. And he and his wife lived happily ever afterwards.

But what became of the goose I never could tell.

By the Brothers Grimm

Snow White and Rose Red

Illustrated by
Gustaf Tenggren

Once there was a poor widow who had two young daughters. They were as lovely as the red and white roses which bloomed beside their cottage door. So their mother called them Snow White and Rose Red.

During the long winters the two girls stayed close by the hearth, keeping their mother's cottage shining neat. In the evenings, when the snow was falling outside their mother would tell them stories.

One evening there came a knock on the door, and when it was opened a great bear poked in his furry brown head.

Snow White and Rose Red were frightened, and they clung to their mother.

Then the bear spoke quietly. 'Do not be afraid,' he said, 'I will do you no harm.'

'Poor bear,' said their mother. 'Come in and lie down by the fire. Take care you do not burn your fur coat.'

So the bear stretched himself before the fire and all night he lay beside the hearth.

In the morning the children let him out, and he disappeared into the woods. But every evening after that he came back to his warm shelter.

When spring came and the forest was green again,
the bear made his farewells.

'All summer I must stay in the forest,' he said. 'All

summer long I must search for my treasure.'
    Then he disappeared among the trees, leaving his
playmates behind.

Soon afterwards, their mother sent Snow White and Rose Red into the woods to gather sticks. There they came upon a dwarf with an old wrinkled face and a long beard. But the end of his beard was caught in the crack of a fallen tree, and he could not pull it free.

Angrily he cried, 'Come and help me!'

The girls tried hard to pull out the beard, but it was too tightly caught.

'There is only one way,' said Snow White. And she pulled out her little pocket scissors and snipped off the end of his beard.

At once, the disagreeable old dwarf snatched up a sack of gold which had been hidden in the tree, and stamped away.

'Stupid girls, to cut off the tip of my beautiful beard! Bad luck to you, I say!'

Not long after, Snow White and Rose Red went fishing. There beside the brook they saw a little figure jumping up and down.

It was the dwarf, with his beard caught in a fishing line, and at the other end of the line was a great fish which was dragging him towards the water.

'Stupid girls!' screamed the dwarf. 'Don't you see the fish is pulling me in? Do something to help!'

The girls tried to untangle beard and line, but they were too tightly entwined.

'There is no other way,' said Rose Red, pulling out her little pocket scissors, and she snipped away the tangled length of beard.

'Now you have really spoiled my looks!' screamed the dwarf. And scooping up a sack of pearls which had lain among the rushes, he stamped away, grumbling.

One day soon after this, the mother sent her two daughters off to the village to buy laces and ribbons and pins. As they were crossing an open rocky field, they heard a pitiful cry.

Running toward the sound, they found a great bird about to carry off the dwarf, who was struggling frantically. The girls snatched at the little man and held him fast until the bird gave up the struggle and flew away.

As soon as the dwarf had recovered his breath, he burst out, 'See what you have done now! See the holes you have torn in my coat with your rough handling, you clumsy creatures!' And with that he shouldered a sack of precious stones and stamped away among the rocks.

The girls were not surprised by his ingratitude, and went on their way to town. But as they crossed the same field, homeward bound, they met the dwarf again.

He had emptied the sack of precious stones on a flat-topped rock and stood admiring their brilliant colours glittering in the evening sun.

Snow White and Rose Red had no sooner stopped to admire them too, than they heard a great growl from the forest behind them, and out came their friend the bear.

At the sight of the bear, the dwarf shook with fright. 'Do not eat me, Mr Bear,' he begged. 'Take my treasure instead – or take these young girls! They will make you a tender meal.'

The angry bear swung out one huge paw; it sent the dwarf spinning over and over through the air, and he never was seen again!

Snow White and Rose Red were frightened, but the bear spoke kindly to them. And as they watched, his bearskin fell from him and slipped to the ground. Then lo and behold! Before them stood a handsome young prince dressed in cloth of gold.

'That dwarf had stolen my treasure and bewitched me,' he explained to the girls. 'Only his death could set me free!'

Very soon Snow White and the prince were married, and his brother married Rose Red. Their mother lived with them in the palace. And before the door she planted her rose trees, which blossomed each year, white and red.

Two Best-loved stories

Illustrated by Gordon Laite

Beauty and the Beast

Once there was a trader who had three daughters. The youngest one was so beautiful that her father called her Beauty. This made her sisters very jealous.

One day good news came to the trader. His ship had finally come into port.

'What shall I bring you?' the father asked his girls.

The oldest daughters asked for fine clothes. Beauty asked only for a rose.

On his way back from town, the trader lost his way in
the woods. Suddenly he saw a great castle surrounded
by flowers. The door was open so he went inside.

The trader saw no one, so he ate and drank and went
to bed. The next day he set out again. On the way he
remembered Beauty's wish and picked a beautiful rose
from the castle garden.

Suddenly there was a loud roar and a fearsome beast rushed up. 'You will die for stealing my rose!' he growled.

'Forgive me,' begged the trader. 'I only took it for one of my daughters. I promised her a rose.'

'Then go home,' the Beast said, 'and send that daughter back to me. Promise me that, and you shall be free.'

'I will gladly go to the Beast,' Beauty said when she heard what had happened, 'otherwise, I would surely die of grief if I caused your death.'

So, to the great joy of her two sisters, Beauty went to the Beast's castle. When she got there, she found a fine table set for dinner.

The Beast came in. 'Did you come here willingly?' he roared.

'Yes,' answered Beauty.

'You are good and I am grateful,' said the Beast. 'Now good night. I will see you tomorrow.'

The next day Beauty wandered all through the castle. Each room was more beautiful than the next. And Beauty's room was the most beautiful of all.

Besides, the Beast had given Beauty a magic mirror through which she could see her home and her father. Her father looked very sad.

That night the Beast came in at dinner time. 'Tell me,' he said, 'do you think I am ugly?'

'Yes,' Beauty answered. 'But you are kind, too. Your kindness makes me forget how ugly you are.'

'I am grateful,' said the Beast. Then he said, 'Beauty, will you marry me?'

BELLE

'No, Beast,' Beauty said softly.

The Beast sighed deeply. 'Then good night,' he said.

Three months passed. Each day the Beast proved his
kindness to Beauty. She had everything she needed.
Each night after dinner, the Beast asked Beauty to
marry him. But Beauty always said, 'No.'

'I don't think I shall ever marry you,' Beauty said
gently. 'But I shall be your friend.'

One day Beauty saw in the magic mirror that her
father was ill. She begged the Beast to let her go home.

'Go,' said the Beast.
'But if you do not come
back after ten days I shall
die of grief.'

Beauty promised she
would come back.

But when she got home
she was so busy she
forgot to count the days.
After she had been away
ten days, Beauty dreamed
that the Beast was dying
of grief.

Beauty woke up. 'Poor
Beast,' she said. 'I have
been so cruel.' She
wished from the bottom
of her heart she was back
in the castle.

The next morning she
was there.

All day Beauty waited impatiently for the night. That
night the Beast did not come to dinner.

Beauty looked everywhere for him. At last she found
the Beast lying in the garden. 'I shall die happy,
because you are back,' the Beast whispered.

'No Beast,' said Beauty. 'Live, and I shall be your
wife.' Then, forgetting his ugliness, Beauty kissed him.

At once, a handsome prince stood where the Beast
had been.

'I was under an evil spell,' the prince explained. 'I
had to remain a beast until a beautiful girl should love
me for my goodness alone.'

The prince took Beauty's hand and led her to the
castle. Beauty found her father there. But her jealous
sisters had been turned to stone statues. Their
punishment was to watch Beauty's happiness until they
too learned to be kind.

Beauty and the prince were married, and they lived
in great happiness.

Rapunzel

Once there was a cottage near to a beautiful garden,
but the man and his wife who lived in the cottage did
not dare go into it because it belonged to a wicked
witch.

One day, the woman noticed in the garden a bed of
fresh radishes. 'Oh, I must have some!' she said to her
husband. 'Unless I can have some I know I shall die!'

The good husband loved his wife very much. That
night he climbed over the wall into the garden and
picked a handful of radishes. But alas, the witch caught
him!

'Thief!' cried the witch. 'How dare you steal my
radishes? You shall pay for this!'

'Be merciful!' begged the man. 'My wife is dying of
longing for your radishes.'

'Very well,' the witch said, 'take all the radishes your
wife can eat. In return you must give your first child to
me.'

Soon after, a baby was born to the pair. The witch
took her away and named her Rapunzel, which means
'radish'. She was a very beautiful child.

When she was twelve, the
witch shut Rapunzel up in
a high tower that had
neither staircase nor door.
When the witch wanted to
come to see her she called,
    'Rapunzel, Rapunzel,
    let down your hair!'
Then Rapunzel unwound
her long golden braids, and
the witch climbed up them.
    With each year,
Rapunzel grew more
beautiful.

One day a handsome prince heard her singing. He
rode to the tower and cried,
  'Rapunzel, Rapunzel,
  let down your hair!'
Then up he climbed. When they saw each other the
prince and Rapunzel immediately fell in love. Rapunzel
promised to marry the prince as soon as she could
escape from the tower.

But the wicked witch discovered the plan. In a rage,
she cut off Rapunzel's hair and sent her off to live in the
wilderness.

Then she waited in the tower to trap the prince. That
evening the prince climbed the golden rope of hair.
Instead of his beloved Rapunzel, he found the horrid
witch.

'Rapunzel is mine!' she screamed. 'You shall die for
trying to steal her!'

The prince leapt from the window, but alas he fell into a thorn bush, and was blinded. For three years he wandered through the woods, weeping for Rapunzel.

But then one day the prince heard someone singing. He walked towards the voice and there was Rapunzel. She wept with joy to see her prince again, and two of her tears fell on his eyes. Instantly he could see!

Then the prince took Rapunzel to his kingdom and they lived happily ever after.

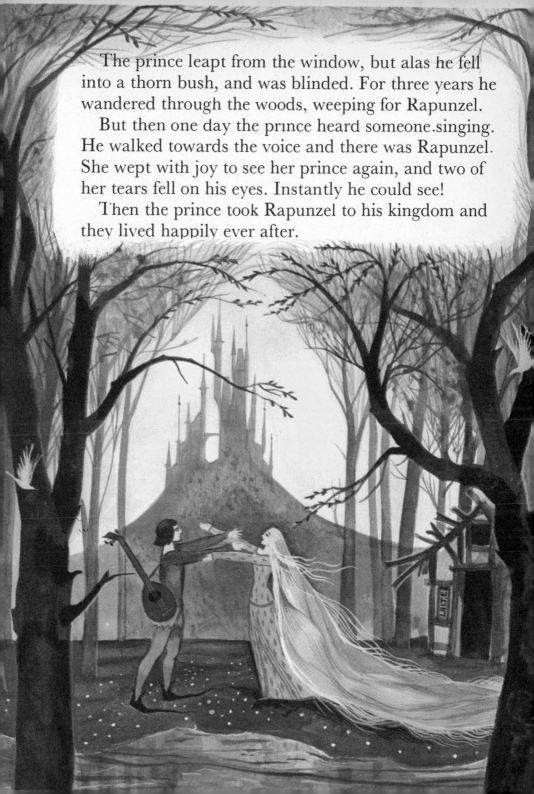

Henny-Penny

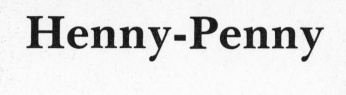

Illustrated by Richard Scarry

One day Henny-Penny was walking through the woods
when 'crack . . . ping!' Something hit her on the head.

'My goodness . . . the sky is falling down! I must go
and tell the king at once!'

She went along and soon she met Cocky-Locky.
'Where are you going, Henny-Penny?' asked
Cocky-Locky.

'The sky is falling down! I am going to tell the king.'

'Can I come with you?' asked Cocky-Locky.

'Certainly,' said Henny-Penny and they both hurried along towards the palace.

On their way they met Ducky-Daddles. 'Where are you going in such a hurry?' he asked.

'Oh, the sky is falling down and we are going to tell the king,' said Henny-Penny and Cocky-Locky.

'Can I come with you?' asked Ducky-Daddles.

'Certainly!' the others agreed, and off they went through the woods together.

So they ran on and eventually they met
Goosey-Poosey.

'Oh, where are you going?' asked Goosey-Poosey.

'We are off to tell the king that the sky is falling
down,' said Henny-Penny, Cocky-Locky and
Ducky-Daddles.

'May I come with you?' asked Goosey-Poosey.

'Yes, of course,' the others all agreed, and so they continued on their way.

Further along the way they met Turkey-Lurkey.

'Where are you going?' asked Turkey-Lurkey.

'The sky is falling down and we are off to tell the king!' said Henny-Penny, Cocky-Locky, Ducky-Daddles and Goosey-Poosey.

'Can I come with you?' asked Turkey-Lurkey.

'Of course you can,' said the others and off they went together.

The next person they met was Foxey-Woxey.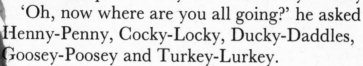

'Oh, now where are you all going?' he asked Henny-Penny, Cocky-Locky, Ducky-Daddles, Goosey-Poosey and Turkey-Lurkey.

'The sky is falling down and we are off as quickly as we can to tell the king!' they all said together.

'But this is not the way to the king,' said Foxey-Woxey. 'I know the real way – shall I show you?'

'Oh, please do,' said Henny-Penny, Cocky-Locky, Ducky-Daddles, Goosey-Poosey and Turkey-Lurkey.

So they followed Foxey-Woxey and he led them to the
entrance of his cave.

'This is the short way to the king's palace,' said
Foxey-Woxey. 'I will go first and you follow me.'

'Oh, most certainly we will!' they all agreed. So
Foxey-Woxey went into his cave, but he didn't go far.

He turned round and waited.
    Along came Turkey-Lurkey – and gulp!
Foxey-Woxey ate up Turkey-Lurkey.

Next came Goosey-Poosey – and gulp! Foxey-Woxey
ate up Goosey-Poosey.

Next came Ducky-Daddles – and gulp! Foxey-Woxey
ate up Ducky-Daddles.

Next came Cocky-Locky – and gulp! Foxey-Woxey
ate up Cocky-Locky.

Last of all came Henny-Penny – and gulp!
Foxey-Woxey ate up Henny-Penny.

So, Foxey-Woxey had eaten all the animals, that were going to see the king – except himself, of course. And Foxey-Woxey had eaten so much that he could hardly move, so he fell asleep by the river.

After all that, the king never found out that the sky was about to fall down on him!

The Little King and the Three Wise Men

By S. Reit

Illustrated by Gordon Laite

Once upon a time there was a little king called Harold.

He wore a golden crown, and over his shoulders, he wore a beautiful golden cloak.

Every day he would sit on his golden throne.

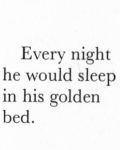

Every night he would sleep in his golden bed.

He brushed
his teeth with a
golden
toothbrush.

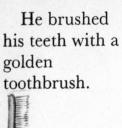

He combed
his hair with a
golden comb.

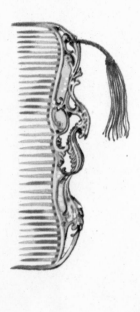

His page boy, Peter, would
bring all the little king's
beautiful golden things when he
needed them.

The three wise men of the
kingdom gave him good advice.

Unfortunately, in spite of having a beautiful golden crown, a golden cloak, golden shoes and all his other golden treasures, the little king Harold never smiled.

Secretly the three wise men talked together. 'Our little king is unhappy,' the first one said.

'Yes. We must make him laugh,' replied the second. 'Take him some new *things*.'

'Yes, something new might amuse him,' replied the first.

They gave him a golden
bassoon so that he could play
music.

They gave him a golden
mirror so that he could look at
himself.

They gave him a pair of
golden ice skates and a set of
golden plates.

They gave him lots of things,

all the golden objects to be
found in the kingdom

But all the time the little king never smiled.

The three wise men just didn't know what to do!

Peter, the page boy, went into the room where the three wise men were talking together.

'Why don't you just ask the king what he would like?' he said to them.

The three wise men looked at him in astonishment.

'We hadn't thought of that,' exclaimed the first.

'We never ask the king anything,' said the second.

'Let's ask him then!' said the third.

So they did.

150

'I've always dreamed of driving a fire engine!' replied the little king.

The three wise men immediately found a fire engine for him. The little king climbed up on the driving seat and away they went. He drove the fire engine as fast as he could, and on the way he lost his golden crown and one of his golden shoes.

But he didn't mind at all. Not at all!

He was smiling!

The Musicians of Bremen

By the Brothers Grimm

Illustrated by J. P. Miller

Once upon a time there was an ass who had served a farmer long and faithfully, but now he was old and his master had decided to get rid of him. When the ass knew about this he ran away. 'I love singing,' he thought. 'I'll go to Bremen and become a musician there.'

On the way he met an old hunting dog who was lying breathless on the road. 'I am running away because my master is going to kill me,' said the dog.

'Come with me,' said the ass. 'I'm going to Bremen to be a musician. You could be one too, because everyone knows how beautiful the cry of the hunting dog is.'

The dog agreed, and together they went along the road until they came to a cat who was sitting in their path, looking very, very sad.

'I am too old to catch mice and my mistress is going to drown me.' said the cat.

'Come to Bremen with us,' said the ass. 'We are going to be musicians. You sing so often at nights, that you would be a good musician too.'

The cat thought that was a splendid idea, and so he joined them. Soon they passed a farmyard where a cock was crowing as loudly as he could. 'My mistress is going to put me in a stew for dinner and I am singing just as long as I can,' said the cock.

'Come with us,' said the ass. 'We are going to Bremen to be musicians. I am sure that with your voice you will have a great success.'

So the cock accepted the invitation and all four of them went on their way. At nightfall they were deep in the forest. The ass and the dog lay down under a big tree, while the cat and the cock settled on the branches.

Just as he was about to close his eyes, the cock saw a bright light in the distance.

'Wake up my friends!' he cried. 'I can see a cottage and a lighted window.'

'Let's go and see what it is,' said the ass. 'Perhaps we can find a better place to spend the night.'

They went towards the cottage and looked through the window.

Can you imagine what they saw? There was a band
of robbers sitting round a table covered with food!

'How nice it would be to have that!' said the cock.

'How can we chase them away?' asked the ass. So the
four animals discussed what to do and decided on a
clever trick. The ass put his feet on the windowsill. The
dog climbed on to his back, then the cat climbed on to
the dog's shoulders, and the cock sat on top of the cat.
When the ass gave a signal they all began to sing at the
tops of their voices. The ass began to bray, the dog to
bark, the cat to meow and the cock to crow. What a
dreadful noise they made!

Then they jumped through the window – making such a din that the robbers were terrified and ran out through the door into the forest!

The four musicians then sat round the table and made a good meal. When they had finished they put out the light.

Soon everything was quiet, and the four companions slept. But down in the forest the robbers began to think that they had run away rather quickly, and when the light disappeared the bravest of them returned to the house.

He went in the door and thinking that everything was calm, he felt for the candle on the table, approached the fireplace and tried to light the candle from the glowing

cinders. But the glowing cinders were the brightly shining eyes of the cat! At once, as he drew near, the cat leapt at his face spitting and clawing.

The terrified robber ran towards the door, but then he tripped over the dog. The dog too leapt up, bit his

leg, and drove him towards the garden. But there was the ass, who began to kick him!

As the robber ran as quickly as he could towards the forest, the cock started crowing loudly from the roof.

At last the robber rejoined the others, very breathless and trembling.

'What has happened?' they cried.

'There is a witch in that house!' said the robber. 'She spat at me, and she scratched me with her nails. Then a man in front of the door slashed me with his knife, and a monster in the garden gave me a thump with a cudgel, and even on the roof there was something crying out, "Take that man away." No, my friends, we cannot go back there.'

So at last the robbers disappeared, leaving behind all their goods and their money. But the cottage was so comfortable for the animal-musicians that they never did get to Bremen. They lived happily in their house in the woods, giving concerts for themselves which they always found absolutely enchanting.